For Peewee

WHILE YOU ARE SLEEPING
A HUTCHINSON BOOK 0 09 189331 3

Published in Great Britain by Hutchinson,
an imprint of Random House Children's Books

This edition published 2006

3 5 7 9 10 8 6 4 2

Copyright © Alexis Deacon, 2006

The right of Alexis Deacon to be identified as
the author and illustrator of this work has been asserted in accordance with
the Copyright, Designs and Patents Act 1988.

RANDOM HOUSE CHILDREN'S BOOKS
61–63 Uxbridge Road, London W5 5SA
A division of The Random House Group Ltd

RANDOM HOUSE AUSTRALIA (PTY) LTD
20 Alfred Street, Milsons Point, Sydney,
New South Wales 2061, Australia

RANDOM HOUSE NEW ZEALAND LTD
18 Poland Road, Glenfield, Auckland 10, New Zealand

RANDOM HOUSE (PTY) LTD
Endulini, 5A Jubilee Road, Parktown 2193, South Africa

THE RANDOM HOUSE GROUP Limited Reg. No. 954009
www.kidsatrandomhouse.co.uk

A CIP catalogue record for this book is available from the British Library.

Printed in China

While You Are Sleeping

Alexis Deacon

HUTCHINSON

London Sydney Auckland Johannesburg

GALWAY COUNTY LIBRARIES

But what's this?
A new toy?

We are the bedside toys.

Do you ever stop to think what we go through,
night after night, to look after you?

All day we sit as still as stone,

waiting, waiting, waiting,

but when the sun goes down
and we're absolutely *sure* you're sleeping . . .

. . . we get up.
We shake our heads.
We stretch our weary legs.
"Another long night
ahead," we say.

He'll have to help us with our work,
if he wants to join our crew.

Each night the whole room
must be checked.

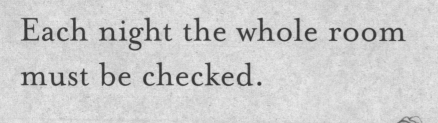

Every cupboard.

Every corner.

We even peek behind the curtains,

and if we're feeling brave . . .

. . . underneath the bed.

But we can't stay long.
There's lots more work for us to do!

If you're too hot,

too cold,

or ill . . .

we try to make it better.

Bed bugs won't bite, we squish them flat.

We scare
bad dreams away.

And on that one night,
when you absolutely must not wake,
we make sure you don't.

We keep you safe no matter what.
That's our job, you see.

If you need us . . .

. . . we'll be there.

And when the sun comes up,
we use our last bit of strength
to crawl back to our places.

Just in time!

Why do we do it?
Why do we put ourselves through it,
night after night after night?
The new toy knows the answer . . .

. . . now he's a bedside toy too.